For more than forty years,
Yearling has been the leading name
in classic and award-winning literature
for young readers.

Yearling books feature children's
favorite authors and characters,
providing dynamic stories of adventure,
humor, history, mystery, and fantasy.

Trust Yearling paperbacks to entertain,
inspire, and promote the love of reading
in all children.

OTHER YEARLING BOOKS YOU WILL ENJOY

THE QUILT

GARY PAULSEN

A Yearling Book

Published by Yearling, an imprint of Random House Children's Books
a division of Random House, Inc., New York

If you purchased this book without a cover you should be aware that this book is stolen property. It was reported as "unsold and destroyed" to the publisher and neither the author nor the publisher has received any payment for this "stripped book."

Copyright © 2004 by Gary Paulsen

All rights reserved. No part of this book may be reproduced or transmitted in any form or by any means, electronic or mechanical, including photocopying, recording, or by any information storage and retrieval system, without the written permission of the publisher, except where permitted by law. For information address Wendy Lamb Books.

Yearling and the jumping horse design are registered trademarks of Random House, Inc.

Visit us on the Web! www.randomhouse.com/kids

Educators and librarians, for a variety of teaching tools, visit us at www.randomhouse.com/teachers

ISBN: 0-440-22936-7

Reprinted by arrangement with Wendy Lamb Books

Printed in the United States of America

October 2005

6 5 4

180-6847

With all love to Hannah

Foreword

This is the third book about my relationship with my grandmother Alida. For various reasons, and to my great good fortune, my grandmother essentially became my mother. The first book, *The Cookcamp*, covered a summer I spent with her when I was just five years old and she was working as a cook for a crew of older men making a road up into Canada from Minnesota during the Second World War. The second, *Alida's Song*, is about the summer I spent with her when I was fourteen.

Initially, because of the pain of remembering the emotional disaster that was my mother, I had decided not to write anything else about my early years with my mother and grandmother; and so in the end of *The Cookcamp* there's a note of finality about seeing my grandmother again when I was a child. But my grandmother shines so in my life, made things so wonderful for me when I was a small boy and, later, when I became a man, that I simply had to write more about her. And so *The Quilt*. All that I am, I am because of her, and in that way this final story, all true, is more hers than mine. By her life, through me, she has made it happen.

In this third book I have just turned six. At six I still did not understand what the war was or how it would affect me. Just two years later I would move to the Philippines and see war personally. I became a street child in Manila, living in the aftermath of the barbaric cruelty the Japanese had committed there. But the summer I was six I learned what women, and more specifically, my grandmother, had to do to keep life, and families, together during the war.

Chapter One

For America, World War II lasted for nearly five years. During those years there was a time when the boy could not live with his mother.

His father had gone off to fight one week after the boy was born and his mother went to work in a munitions factory in Chicago. At first the boy lived with her in the tiny apartment by the elevated railway. Soon, though, other people—men—came to visit her and she started to do very grown-up things. He did not fit in, and when life with his mother became too difficult, he went to live with his grandmother.

The first time this happened his grandmother was

working as a cook for a group of men building a war road from northern Minnesota up into Canada. They spent a wonderful summer together; later he would remember only good things about those months and indeed all the times he was with his grandmother.

He called her Grandma. Her name was Alida but he called her Grandma and he loved her very much, as he would love her the rest of her life and his life, and she adored him as well and cooked him apple pies and knitted stockings and mittens for him even though it was summer and read him letters from his mother, which made him love his mother, even though sometimes he would look at the paper his grandmother held and see that there was no writing on it. And she spoke to him in Norwegian as if he were a little man and not a boy.

The second time he went to live with his grandmother he was just six and he stayed with her at first in her small house in a little town near the Canadian border, in Minnesota.

There were only a hundred and forty people living in this town and he lived with her in a two-room house that was set on the outskirts of the village near a small stream. The water made a wonderful burbling noise that helped him sleep when he thought of his mother in Chicago and missed her.

Once, while his grandmother was sitting at the small table in the one room that served as parlor, living room and kitchen, he asked her, "If I miss Mother so much"—and he called her Mother then, although when he spoke to his mother he always called her Mom—"why is it that I can't be with her?"

And his grandmother, who was crocheting what would become a bedspread, put her crocheting down on her lap. She took him in her arms, which he always liked but did not see a reason for now, and said, "She is living in a very fast time, your mother, and working very hard, and she would not have time to spend with you and that would make her sad. It's bad to be sad."

"Sometimes in the night when I think of her and miss her *I'm* sad."

"I know, I know. And that is why you're with me. That's just the way things are now."

"Is it because of the war?"

"Yes. It's the war."

"I thought it was because of the men who came home with her from the plant where they make bullets for the soldiers."

"No. Those men are nothing and you mustn't think about them."

"Do they come home with her because of the war?"

"Yes. They are nothing to think about." And she went back to her crocheting except that he could see that her fingers went very fast and hard with the crochet hook, and she missed a stitch and had to go back. He could tell that she was upset but could not understand why and thought it was something he'd said, and hugged her and stood next to her that way for several moments. Then he said, because he thought it would help, "I don't miss my father at all."

Her fingers stopped for a moment, then continued, more slowly, and she sighed. "You never saw him. He was in the deserts in California training in tanks when you were born and they sent him right overseas."

"But I will see him someday."

"Yes."

"After the war."

4

"Yes, after the war."

He thought for another moment. "When will the war be over?"

Her fingers stopped again and her voice grew tight and with the clipped sound of her Norwegian accent had almost knife edges. "When men are sick and tired of being men . . ." She trailed off. "Never mind. The war will be over when it's over. Go play outside."

It was summer and he played on the edge of the water and in the stream, which was only ankle-deep, making boats with leaves and sticks and lying down on his side to make them look bigger so they were like ships as they bounced and careened down the rapids. Enemy ships, which he had seen in newsreels on the rare occasions when his mother had taken him to Gene Autry and Roy Rogers movies in Chicago, which he liked very much—the movies—even though he did not know exactly what an enemy was except that one was German and one was Japanese and he did not know exactly what *they* were except that they were bad and soldiers were fighting them.

He played war with the stick boats and leaf ships

and dropped rocks on them and pretended they were bombs, and each time he sank one of them he pretended he was helping his father in some way, by killing the Germans and Japanese, and he would be able to come home and send away the men who visited the boy's mother in Chicago.

He would sometimes play in the stream all day until his grandmother called him in to eat. He would find that it was very late and still light and his eyes could barely stay open.

They ate potatoes and small pieces of venison that his grandmother got from neighbors who hunted deer. And she made him apple pies, as she had in the cookcamp in the woods the year before. Sometimes they had *lefsa*, a kind of big tortilla made of potato flour, which she cooked on a piece of iron on top of the stove.

The *lefsa* was delicious, especially when she smeared it with butter and rolled it into a long tube with chokecherry jelly she had made from berries picked in the summer.

Sometimes he would find himself in her lap, falling

asleep with *lefsa* in his mouth and the sun still bright outside.

"Why is the sun still out at night here? It's not in Chicago," he asked one day, sitting at the table. "Is it because of the war?"

She shook her head and smiled. "No. God makes the days long in summer in the north so Norwegians have more time to get all their work done."

"What's a Norwegian?"

She laughed. "Why you are, little one. You're my brave little Norwegian." And she sang a song about a thousand Swedes who ran through the weeds with one Norwegian chasing them, and he didn't understand really what it meant but tried to hum along with her.

She sang a lot in that time when the two of them lived in the little house and most of his memories of then would have her singing. She sang short songs with a foreign sound, which he would find was Norwegian. She sang while she cooked, leaning over the stove with flour on her cheeks and in her hair, her eyes crinkled with smiles.

One day she decided to hang new wallpaper in the

little bedroom and she made paste with flour and water and took out the wallpaper with the pretty flowers that she had ordered from Sears and Roebuck. A neighbor lady came to help. Her name was Clair and she was old like his grandmother and had the same lines by her eyes from smiling all the time. She brought a quart jar full of red liquid that she said was her special berry wine.

He had often seen his mother drinking beer in the Cozy Corner Bar in Chicago when she met with men. She'd have him stand on the bar and sing the "Mares eat oats and goats eat oats and little lambs eat ivy" song, which he always got wrong and sang, "Marzeedotes and goazeedotes and liddlamseetdivey."

Everybody laughed when he sang and gave him drumsticks of Southern fried chicken and nickel bottles of Coca-Cola. He liked all that, but he didn't like what the drinking did to his mother.

But his grandmother and Clair were different. They took little sips from jelly glasses and even gave him a little sip, which tasted sweet and a bit sticky, and soon they were giggling and flopping the wallpaper over their heads when they tried to hang it, and his grandmother began singing songs that made Clair blush, even though when they weren't laughing she sang along.

The wallpaper never did get pasted to the walls, and instead his grandmother and Clair sat in the kitchen and talked about when they were young. The boy sat listening because they laughed the whole time they talked, and he thought how much fun they must have had when they were young.

"I should have married Clarence," Clair said once.

"He didn't ask you," his grandmother said, laughing, "he asked me. And I married him. You married Sven, remember?"

"Yes, Alida," Clair said, "but Sven was weak and Clarence was strong."

"You had three sons with Sven before he died."

"But you had four, Alida, and four daughters, before Clarence passed on. . . ."

"That's true. But even so, you loved Sven, didn't you?"

"Sven was a poet," Clair said, nodding, but then she smiled and added, "But poets don't always get the wood cut, if you know what I mean."

And his grandmother laughed and blushed and said, "Oh, you, Clair, you're terrible!"

And they laughed and laughed, sipping the sticky wine, and the boy didn't understand most of what they said. As the evening came on he kept closing his eyes and opening them more slowly, and he finally felt himself being carried to bed and thought if his mother was this way when she drank he would not mind it so much.

The next morning the sound of his grandmother slamming pans in the kitchen woke him up and he went out in his pajamas to see her making pancakes.

"This morning," she said, all smiles, "we are having buttermilk pancakes fried in bear grease with honey on top."

"What's bear grease?" he asked, rubbing his eyes.

"It's grease made from bears. Clair brought two quarts of it over when she came to help with the papering and I thought you might like to taste pancakes made with it. It's the very best for pancakes and doughnuts and rubbing on your boots."

And while he tried to think of how you could get

grease from a bear or why you would use it for pan-cakes or doughnuts or why you would rub it on your boots, his grandmother's ring came from the phone hanging on the wall.

He loved the party line. In the city everybody had their own private phone but here all the phones were on the same line and each had their own special ring. His grandmother's ring was a short, a long and then another short, but they heard all the rings and often his grandmother would put her hand over the mouth-piece and hold the earpiece to her ear and listen in on other people's conversations.

It was called rubbernecking, and he loved it even though his grandmother said it was wrong.

"But you do it," he said.

"Yes, but it's still wrong, and it's very wrong for you, my little Norwegian."

But this time the ring was for her and she wiped the flour from her hands and took the earpiece from the hook on the side and rose on her toes to reach the mouthpiece.

"Hello, yes, this is Alida!" She always yelled in the

telephone and she started every sentence with "Hello, yes," as if she needed to constantly reestablish that she was still there listening. "Hello, yes, Kristina, go ahead!"

The boy heard only the one side, though he listened hard.

"Hello, yes, I see."

And: "Hello, yes, that will be fine. How soon?"

And: "Hello, yes, I'll have to get Elmer to give us a ride out. It depends on his truck. With the gas rationing he has to run it on tractor fuel and sometimes he can't keep it running. We'll see you when we see you."

She listened again, then: "Hello, yes, there's no problem. He's a good boy and no trouble. Yes, then, we'll see you."

And she hung up and turned to the boy and smiled and said, "We're going to go spend some time with Kristina. Her man is off in the war and she needs some help on her farm."

Which is how it happened that the boy learned of the quilt.

Chapter Two

The boy had not been raised on a farm. Most of his life he had been in Minneapolis, living in a small apartment with his mother while she worked at a laundry and then in another small apartment in Chicago when she went to work at the munitions factory. He knew a little about city living, about how to say "hello" and "please" and "thank you" to the super, how not to make noise in the hallways, how to play in one place so his mother could find him easily, how not to make noise when his mother napped because she worked the night shift, how not to go outside the building because there were bad men, how to turn the radio on and listen to the Lone Ranger and Edgar Bergen and Charlie McCarthy and Red Skelton, how to be careful of Mr. McAllister, who lived next door and did not like children.

But he knew almost nothing of farms. He had seen farms when he visited his cousins at Christmas for a day or two but had no real concept of what happened on one and so he was very excited all through the evening while his grandmother packed.

"Is it a big farm?"

"Not so large. I think they have a hundred and sixty acres with about eighty acres cleared."

"Does she have animals?"

"Of course, silly. All farms have animals."

"What kind of animals?"

She looked at him. "Farm animals."

"Are there cows?"

She held up a denim jacket that had seen better days, then shrugged and put it in the box she was packing. "Yes, cows."

"And horses?"

"Of course. You can't farm without workhorses. Who would do the work?"

"Chickens?"

"Yes. Chickens and ducks and horses and cows and pigs. All the farm animals." She sighed as she put a worn dress in the box. "Now, get ready for bed. Elmer is coming to get us early in the morning to take us out to Kristina's farm and we have to be rested and ready."

He put on his pajamas and she washed his face and tucked him into the small cot next to her bed, but at first he was too excited to sleep. He listened to her moving around, packing, and just as he started to doze off he remembered something.

"Will she have a dog?" he called.

"A dog, yes. And cats, too, I suspect. She might even have fish or a kangaroo. Now go to *sleep*."

But still sleep wouldn't come and he turned and tossed, until at last his eyes closed for just a second. Then he heard his grandmother say, "Come on, sleepy bones, Elmer will be here soon and we have to have breakfast ready for him."

It was hard to decide on who was older or in worse shape, Elmer or his truck. In the layers of family in the north part of Minnesota, where it seemed that almost everybody was related in some way, Elmer was some distant relation to the boy's grandmother but older, much older, than her and broken by his years.

He was short and bent, with an old wool jacket that seemed almost to reach the ground, and a beard that was gray and roughly cut with a scissors, and tufts of hair that grew thickly out of both ears and both nostrils.

The top of his head was completely bald and around the sides there was a white ring of silver-gray hair that he apparently also kept trimmed with the same hacking scissors he used on his beard.

There was not a tooth in his head and he had long ago broken what served as his dentures so that he had callused gums that were so hard he could actually chew, and the boy watched with outright fascination as he ate pancakes. His manners were fastidious and he carefully dabbed at his mouth with a handkerchief after each bite, and when he had finished eating he sipped coffee into which he dipped two sugar lumps, which he put inside his lower lip while drinking the coffee.

He then turned to the boy's grandmother and said something that seemed completely made up of lisps and whispers. The boy could not understand a word, but apparently his grandmother could because she turned to the boy and said, "Get your travel bag and go out to the truck. We have to leave. It's a long way and his truck is acting up."

"He said all that?"

"Of course," she said. "In perfect Norwegian. Now, hurry. Elmer is a busy man. He's the only one around with a truck that can take us anywhere. All the rest of the men are in the war."

The boy took his small tote bag, which he had used to carry his three favorite toys from Chicago: a small stuffed dog that he'd had since he was little (that was how he thought of it, had since he was little); a rubber statue of the Lone Ranger and his horse, Silver, the heroes of his favorite radio show; and a little metal tank, which he kept because his father was in tanks.

With the bag over his shoulder he went out into the summer morning to get into the truck. He stepped out of the door and stopped.

It was a truck in name only. Somewhere in the past—the ancient past, because the truck actually had wooden-spoke wheels—Elmer had taken a car, a four-door sedan, and cut the roof and doors off and made a wooden-plank bed that came up to the rear of the front seat and hung out the back over what might have once been a rear bumper. There was no roof, no stuffing left in the seat—Elmer had put two burlap sacks over the bare springs sticking up—and the wind-shield, which provided a minimum of protection, was such a maze of cracks and chips that it was impossible to see through it.

And then, as a finishing touch, for twenty or so years Elmer had hauled loads of wood, straw, feed, dead animals, live animals, dirt, concrete—countless loads of everything imaginable—and each load had left a deposit of some kind on the planks.

"Where am I going to sit?" the boy asked.

Elmer rattled off some words to his grandmother and

she said to the boy, "Just sit on the boards in back of the seat."

"They're covered with potty." He knew the other word, had heard his mother say it many times, but also knew he would get in trouble for saying it. "It's everywhere."

She looked and then shrugged. "It's just chicken manure. It will wash out. Go ahead and sit down—you'll be walking barefoot in it before long."

"In *potty*?"

She laughed. "It will squeeze up between your toes like mud. You'll like it. It's good for you."

"*Potty?*" he repeated, but she was stuffing boxes and bags in back of the seat. When she was finished he climbed onto the top of the pile and sat down—far away from the potty. Elmer moved levers on the steering wheel. Then, with further lisping and loud hissing (his grandmother reached around and covered the boy's ears), he went to the front of the vehicle and, using a crank and more swearing (the boy was sure it was swearing, because some of the words had the same sound in any language), he cranked and jiggled and levered until the truck gave a loud gasp of smoke, hesitated and finally started wheezing into life.

Elmer ran around the truck, worked the levers some more—there was no foot accelerator and the throttle was a lever on the steering wheel—and with further sputtering and coughing and grinding sounds the truck started moving down the road in an absolutely blinding cloud of smoke.

On top of everything else the truck had no muffler. The explosions from the four cylinders, when they chose to fire, was deafening.

Elmer leaned over and screamed something to him. His grandmother turned and nodded at Elmer and yelled to the boy, "He said that usually it runs better. A little better. It's just that he has to use low-grade tractor fuel and that's why it's so rough and smoky." She turned and looked out through the cracked windshield, then looked back at the boy again and smiled.

"What a nice day for a drive. We'll be there in no time at all."

Chapter Three

The ride was more in the nature of an adventure than something that would take "no time at all."

Initially the road was just a single gravel lane cut through the forest, and then it turned into simple dirt, wide enough for one vehicle, with a ditch cut on each side and thick trees interspersed with small man-made clearings of forty to eighty acres.

Had it been raining, or winter, or spring, they would not have been able to travel at all; with mud or snow the track would have been completely impassable.

As it was, the highest speed the truck could maintain was ten miles an hour. Kristina's farm was only seven miles away. But age, wear on machinery and the poor quality of tractor fuel, which was little more than low-grade kerosene, all contributed to slow the truck to a measly four or five miles an hour—hardly more than walking speed. Indeed, on more than one occasion the boy and his grandmother got out and walked alongside the bouncing vehicle. Every quarter to half mile the engine would overheat and Elmer would have to stop the truck, let the engine cool down and get a bucket of water from the ditch to pour into the boiled-over radiator. Each of these stops took half an hour or so and the end result was that the truck averaged about a mile an hour.

The boy loved it. In his mind it was a grand adventure, a voyage through wilderness, and he imagined wild beasts and Indians and even Germans and Japanese hiding in the forest along the road. He found a stick in the shape of a gun and used it to guard and defend the truck and Elmer and his grandmother. As they churned past each new homestead, which is what the small clearings were, the people who turned to look and the children who ran out to see them became the people who cheered the tanks that liberated villages in the newsreels.

He felt very much the hero, and when, nearly seven hours after they started, they came to a wooden mailbox with the name Olaf Jorgenson carved on the side, he felt almost sad that it was over.

The driveway was a tunnel through overhanging thick green trees and brush. They drove through them, bouncing and jerking with steam boiling out of the radiator, for two hundred yards until they came to a clearing. To the left stood a small, neat two-story white-painted frame house, surrounded by a low white wooden fence. To the right stood a series of smaller buildings—a granary, a chicken coop, a shed and a red barn with an arched roof. Next to the barn was an old Minneapolis-Moline tractor with steel lug wheels, all covered with rust, and next to that, a wagon with high sides and a long wooden tongue that stuck out the front and lay on the ground.

There was no other machinery, no car, no truck. As they hammered-wheezed-smoked into the yard a cloud of chickens exploded into running flight and a dog came streaking out from in back of the barn barking, with his shoulder hair up.

Elmer tried to kill the engine. Of course, now it refused to die. He jerked the throttle and spark levers down and he had to engage the hand clutch to lunge it ahead to still the yammering.

There was a moment of silence, deafening after seven hours of noise. In the sudden quiet, broken only by the barking dog and cackling chickens, his grandmother said:

"We're at last here."

The boy was out of the truck instantly and the dog, after peeing on the tire, approached him with tail wagging and pushed against his leg. He knelt and hugged it and began petting it while Elmer stiffly got out and his grandmother turned and handed boxes and sacks to Elmer.

There was still no other indication that people lived at the farm.

When their packages were on the ground Elmer went to the front of the truck and turned the crank to start it. He climbed on, made a big circle in the dusty barnyard and disappeared down the driveway, the truck clanking and smoking.

The dog broke away to chase the truck. The boy stood up.

"He didn't say goodbye."

"Yes, he said it in Norwegian, but not loud. You must not say it loud or the devil will hear and ruin your trip. He had to hurry to get back before dark."

"Does the devil come in the dark?"

"No. He doesn't have any lights."

"The devil?"

"No. Elmer."

The truck had disappeared, but the boy could still hear it. "But can't the devil hear the truck anyway?"

"That's different. Come now, grab a box and let's get up to the house."

Just then the screen door slammed. A woman came out of the porch along the front of the house.

She was very tall, wearing large men's bib overalls and a blue work shirt, with long white-blond hair tied up in a bun on her head, and she was hugely pregnant.

"Why is her belly so big?" the boy asked in a whisper.

"She's going to have a baby," his grandmother said. "Very soon. That's why we're here. To help."

Kristina came through the gate and stopped. "Alida! It's so good to see you! And I see you brought your helper. I would have come out sooner but I was putting bread in the oven. Why did Elmer leave so soon? Usually he stays to eat."

"He wants to get back before dark," Alida answered. "Though if he knew you had fresh bread he might have stayed. That man loves his gullet."

Kristina had a big voice, strong but still soft in some way, and she leaned down and shook the boy's hand and he saw her face close on for the first time and thought, and would think for the rest of his life, that she was the most beautiful woman he had ever seen.

Her eyes were a striking blue and almond-shaped, with a tilt at the corners and long blond lashes. Her nose had a slight upturn and her teeth were even and white when she smiled at him. He liked her instantly.

"We're here," he said, "to help you have a baby."

"Hush!" his grandmother said. "How you talk!"

"Well, that's what you said. Just now, you said we were here to help."

"Sometimes the young ones talk just to hear themselves," his grandmother said. "Hush now."

"But—"

"Well, he's right, Alida. That's why you came out here. Come now, to the house, before the banty roosters come out of the coop and make a fuss. They think they own the world and don't like company, and we have to eat supper before chores."

Kristina picked up a box and went to the house and the boy and his grandmother followed with the rest of their packages.

"I have a room in the back for you and the boy," Kristina said, "and a cradle for the baby, which will be good for a while. He can lie with me when he first comes."

"He?"

"I did the flour-and-ring test last night and three times it pointed to boy. That's what Olaf wants most. A boy. It would be so nice to surprise him with a son when he comes home."

27

She stopped talking and the boy thought it was because they were at the door, but he caught a glimpse of her face and saw she was crying, soft tears, and it didn't make sense to him until she said:

"The damn war. The damn, damn war."

"Men," his grandmother said. "It's how they fix things. Fight over them. Just like bulls."

When they entered the house, they came directly into the kitchen. The boy immediately smelled the bread baking and started to salivate. Except for a jar of canned wild plums they had opened on the way and shared with Elmer, they had not eaten all day, and he was starved.

Along one wall was a wood-burning cookstove, facing the door, and it was making the room very hot because Kristina had it fired up to bake the bread. On the other wall, to the right, there was a sink, but instead of faucets it had a hand pump. To the left the wall was full of cupboards.

In the middle of the kitchen was a table with four wooden chairs, and from the ceiling hung a Coleman gas lantern. There was no electricity on the farm. But that summer in the cookcamp the boy and his grand-mother had lived without electricity, so he knew about lanterns and candles.

"Sit," Kristina said. "We'll eat."

"Let me," his grandmother said, moving to the cup-boards. "You're so close now. Let me do the work."

"But I feel fine."

"Hush now," his grandmother said. "Don't let the devil hear."

"Oh, Alida . . ."

They put the boxes and packages in a side room. Soon there were plates and silverware on the table. His grandmother cut fresh bread, hot from the oven, and took a jar of honey from the cupboard and from the top of the stove a cast-iron pot filled with stew. They sat to eat.

They did not talk while they sat but kept at the food until they were done. The boy ate three slices of hot bread with sugared honey and a full plate of stew and thought he had never eaten food that tasted so won-derful, and when they were done they put the dishes in the sink for later and went back out into the yard.

It was still light and with the summer sun would be light for another four hours. The boy was halfway across the barnyard, following his grandmother and Kristina and looking for the dog when he heard a loud chukkering behind him. He turned to see four enraged banty roosters, with their neck feathers all puffed up, flying through the air toward his head.

"Grandma!" he yelled, and ran for her skirts. She turned and waved her arms.

"Get gone with you, damn you!"

And the roosters seemed to stop in midair. They veered off to the side and backed away.

"They're cowards," Kristina said over her shoulder without turning. "Just don't let them bluff you down."

"What's bluff?" The boy watched them flutter from the protection of his grandmother's skirt.

"Like a lie," his grandmother said. "They lie to scare you and pretend they're tough, but they're all talk."

They didn't look like all talk to the boy. They looked like they could tear his head off and he decided either he would not come into the yard alone or he would find a big stick to carry. Faced with Alida, however, the roosters gave up and moved off to the back of the barn to look for bugs in the manure.

The barn was a wonderful mystery to the boy, dark and cool. Three cats came up and rubbed their sides against his legs in greeting.

"Cotton, Candy," said Kristina, pointing at two gold cats, and then at a brown one, "and Mud. We got them to keep the rats and mice down but they mostly just steal milk."

She moved to the back of the barn and slid the door open. The boy was surprised to see seven cows standing there, waiting to come into the barn.

"Hello, girls," Kristina said. She turned back into the barn and the cows followed her in. They were enormous and the boy moved back against the front wall. But they all trooped to their stalls, each waiting for the one next to her to get settled before going into her own stall.

"They know where to go," he said. "Just like people . . ."

"Better than people." His grandmother snorted as she carried a bucket from a little side room. She took a stool from a hook on the wall, leaving two other small three-legged stools. "They almost never fight. . . . People aren't so smart."

The boy remembered suddenly. "What was that word she used back in the house?"

"What word?"

"She said 'shores,' or 'chores.' What does that mean?"

"It means light work," she said, smiling down at him. "Light work in the mornings and evenings before the real work starts. . . . You'll see. Now, here, carry this stool down to that red cow on the end. We'll start there and Kristina can come the other way and we'll meet in the middle."

Chapter Four

The boy did not think of it as light work. Kristina might be pregnant but she could work like a man, and his grandmother and Kristina kept him running.

"Your job is to carry the stools between the cows for us," Kristina said, smiling as she finished milking a cow. She stood to carry the bucket of milk to the milk cans in the pump room at the end of the bar.

"I could carry the buckets of milk," he said. She shook her head. "Not yet. Just the stools for now, and keep the cats from sitting on top of the cows. Abigail and Eunice don't like it and they fidget and give less milk."

"The cows have names?"

"You bet. And they know them." She slapped the cow she had just finished milking lightly on the rump. "Isn't that right, Abby?" And the cow turned and looked at her before turning back to face forward.

They didn't quite meet in the middle. His grandmother did four cows and Kristina did only three, but twice the boy saw her stop milking and lean her head into the cow's flank and close her eyes and wince and sigh, and he guessed that something about having a baby was hard work and perhaps hurt or made a person tired and he decided to work as hard as he could and help as much as he could.

He ran back and forth with the stools and tried to shoo the cats off the cows but they ignored him. When milking first started, they sat up on their hind legs like little bears in back of his grandmother and Kristina and waited to have milk squirted into their mouths. But soon they'd had enough milk, and they jumped up onto the backs of the cows and began jumping from cow to cow, playing on them.

Some of the cows did fidget, and while at first he was afraid because the cows were so large, after a time he realized how gentle they were and he went between them after the cats. Soon he ignored the cows completely.

What with chasing cats, running back and forth with the stools and then after the cats, by the time milking was done and all the milk put into the milk cans in the water trough in the pump room, the boy was so tired he nearly staggered as they walked back to the house.

In the kitchen he found they were to eat again, a light lunch (as his grandmother called it) before going to bed. He sat in a chair at the table.

It had been a long day, with Elmer and the truck and the road and getting to the farm and milking and learning about roosters and cats jumping on cows and wagging dogs and cows with names and Kristina, and soon his eyes closed and no matter what he did he could not get them to open again, food or no food. The last thing he remembered was his grandmother carrying him, saying, "What a good little man you are," and putting him into a bed with a feather mattress so soft he just sank and sank until he thought he would never come up and then, just, plain, nothing.

Morning.

He opened his eyes because bright sun was coming through a window across his face, and he heard something he had never heard before, the sound of a rooster crowing.

He lay for a moment, still half asleep, remembering where he was, thinking of the day before and his mother, wondering if she'd ever seen cows and geese and chickens, and he heard the two women talking in the kitchen, just off the bedroom where he lay.

"It started while we were milking this morning but I'm not sure about time, Alida. He was home on leave for two weeks and it seems like we spent most of it in the sheets. It could have been any time in those two weeks."

"So what's the soonest, and the latest?"

"Three days ago was soonest . . . nine or ten days from now would be the latest."

"And you waited until day before yesterday to call me?"

"I didn't want to be a bother."

"Babies are never a bother. We have to call Martha."

"But I haven't any pains yet; my water hasn't broken—"

"Kristina, I'm not a midwife. We have to call Martha. She knows what to do and it might take her a day or two to get her own things in order to come over here. I'll call her after lunch."

"But—"

"There will be none of the buts. I know what they say, first come, late come. But you're so big. . . . We'll call Martha right away. And I'm going to call some of the other girls too. Sometimes you can't have too many women."

A lot of it made no sense to the boy and he felt bad that he had missed morning milking and they had let him sleep. But he knew they were talking about the baby and when it might come, and he was excited at the prospect because he did not know anything about how babies came or what you did or how they worked except that it must be inside Kristina and had to come out, and he had many questions he wanted to ask.

But his grandmother's voice sounded tight and worried, the way it did when he asked bad questions about his mother. So he decided to hold back. He rolled out of bed and went into the kitchen and asked instead, "Where's the potty?" He hadn't seen a bathroom. Both women laughed and Kristina said, "Outside, in back of the house, there's a little house with a seat with holes in it. Just rip a page out of the catalog for paper. Or if it's just front potty you can go in the bushes."

He had gone to the bathroom outside when he was at the cookcamp with his grandmother, just number one (he had never heard "front potty" before) and they had had a potty chair in the trailer. This was more serious than number one and he went outside and found the little house. He did his business, wondering while he was sitting there why they called it number one and number two. He stood and opened the door to see the roosters, all four of them, standing there staring at him, chukkering with their neck feathers out in threat. He closed the door.

At first he was frightened and chagrined that he had forgotten them. The dog, who was named Jake and who had apparently followed the boy from the house, sat there too, watching the roosters, his ears cocked. After a time the boy collected himself, remembering what they'd told him about the roosters being cowards. He opened the door, raised his arms wide to make himself look bigger, screamed "Yaaaaahhhhh!" and ran right at them.

It was most gratifying. They were taken completely by surprise and as a bonus, Jake joined in the fun. Feathers flew as the roosters squawked and screeched out of the yard, the dog on their tails, and the boy almost strutted back into the house, his pajamas flopping.

"I ran into the roosters," he said, sitting at the table. "Me and the dog had to chase them out of the yard."

But the two women weren't listening. Kristina was standing, leaning against the wall, her face pale and drawn, and his grandmother was on the phone, cranking the one long ring that would get Central.

"You must go outside," she told him, holding her hand over the mouthpiece, "and play alone for a little time. We have something to do now."

"Is it the baby?" he asked.

"Play. Go play outside now, hurry," and then, turning to the phone, she said, "Central, this is Alida out to Kristina's. Get Martha out here as soon as possible and tell her to bring the others. It's starting."

Chapter Five

Women came from everywhere. He had been in the yard for only a short time, making roads in the dust with a small wooden blade that he pretended was the bulldozer he had ridden the summer before at the cookcamp, when the first wagon came down the driveway from the road.

He had not seen horses pull before and he was amazed by the team that came with the first freight wagon. There were two of them, one gray with white markings on his forehead and the other all brown, and they were huge, like living walls of horses pulling into the yard. They had come at a trot and were covered with sweat and surrounded by flies. Two women holding cloth bags and what looked like folded sheets climbed down from the high seat in front of the box, using the steel spokes of the wheels as steps. They left a boy in the seat holding the reins, a boy who did not seem that much older than he was.

He hoped the boy would stay to play, but instead the driver expertly slapped the reins against the rumps of the horses and they obediently pulled in a wide circle. Without waving or saying anything he started back down the driveway.

One of the women called after him. "You stop and water them in a ditch and let them blow, and don't you run them. You and your sister take care of the chores until I come back. I'll be home when I get there." The other woman smiled and waved.

With that they made their way to the house.

Perhaps an hour passed, and the boy was very curious about what was happening but just as he decided to go inside or at least peek through the door, another wagon, pulled by two similar horses, both sweaty, came trotting down the drive. This time three women got off and went inside and a girl who was perhaps ten or eleven sat holding the reins. She called after one of the women:

"I should stay and help."

One of the women turned. She was plump and wearing an old-time dress that came almost to the ground, and she had red cheeks and dark hair up in a bun. "Not this time," she said. "You're too young yet. You go home and tend to chores."

"How am I ever going to learn?" the girl asked.

"You're too young," the woman repeated, and then one of the other women pulled at her arm and said:

"Come on, Martha, let's get inside."

With that the three women disappeared into the house and the girl turned the horses and wagon, as expertly as the previous boy had done, and the team walked down and out the driveway. The boy watched and thought of numbers. He liked to work numbers in his head and he thought, All right, there's Kristina and my grandmother, that's two, and then two women in the first wagon, that makes three, and four, and then three women in the last wagon, that makes five and six and seven.

He looked at the house and he thought of seven

women in there and how small the house was and where would he sleep? Then he heard a familiar slamming and wheezing and banging, and he looked up to see Elmer's truck coming down the drive and next to Elmer was another woman.

Whereas the rest of the women had been younger, she was old, like his grandmother, and she stepped out of Elmer's truck stiffly, holding a large bag, made from sheet material, that contained some kind of folded colored patches, and a smaller burlap sack that seemed to be filled with jars.

Elmer waved to the boy and smiled a toothless grin but like the wagons he did not stay, instead turning the truck and hammering back down the driveway.

There was a moment of silence and the woman looked at the boy. "You must be Eunice's boy, visiting with Alida?"

He nodded. "She's my grandma."

"Well I'm her cousin Gerta, so that makes us . . . I don't exactly know. Third or fourth cousins. But we're related. We're *all* related, I guess. Here, carry this sack of jars for me. This quilt is so bulky."

44

He took the heavy sack gladly. It proved to be full of jars of canned food. He was dying to get into the house and see what was happening, but once he did he was disappointed. It was just all noise.

Women filled the kitchen. The stove was fired up and in the heat everybody was sweating and all of them seemed to be talking at once, and not a word of it was English but was all Norwegian, and it meant nothing to him, just sounds mixed with banging and rattling from pans on the stove and the creaking of the pump handles.

He moved to a corner, out of the way, and they all ignored him except one woman, who had blond hair and blue eyes like Kristina but was not as young or quite as pretty. She smiled at him and gave him a slab of bread covered with butter and honey. He ate it wolfishly, realizing that it was well past lunchtime. Then he went to the pump, where a dipper hung on a hook, and held the dipper up to another woman, who pumped it full and handed it to him without really looking at him, speaking in Norwegian to a woman by the stove all the while.

He did not see either his grandmother or Kristina—
or the woman called Martha—and stood back in the
corner sipping, and guessed that his grandmother and
Kristina and Martha were in the upstairs bedroom,
which he had not seen. Then he heard the sound.

It was not, quite, a scream. He would grow to be
something of a man and be in the army and later work
on an ambulance and, somehow, live to become an
older man, and he would see and hear and do many
cutting and bad things but he would never, ever, hear
anything like that sound.

It came from upstairs but seemed to fill the whole
house, a deep, grunting, ripping sound that turned into
a piercing shriek and ended in panting murmurs.

For a second the talking in the kitchen stopped and
the boy was truly horrified, wondering how Kristina
(he guessed she was the one who made the sound)
could have lived through such a thing.

But then, to his even deeper horror, the women
went back to talking. One of them said in English,
"She's starting to push now. Maybe it won't be long."

"First ones take forever," another said. And then

added, "Easy to make, hard to take," and everybody laughed and they started talking again, but as though a change had happened they did not speak only in Norwegian but mixed the talk with English.

The boy could not believe they were joking about that sound. He could not believe anybody would joke about the sound he heard coming out of that upstairs bedroom and he turned and started for the door, thinking he would rather be outside, walking, when the sound came again. Louder.

"They're close together," one woman said. "She's pushing. Very soon . . ."

"Very soon," another said, and they all nodded as though the sound, which cut the boy to the center, meant nothing. He ran from the kitchen out into the yard by the gate and sat there petting the dog, trying not to hear what came from the house.

Chapter Six

He did not see his grandmother all day and when it came time for milking, two of the other women came out with the buckets and he went to the barn to help.

They were both nice to him, but they carried their own stools and he spent most of the time chasing the cats from the cows' backs. On one of his runs after a cat, he got to the back door of the barn and came face to face with a team of workhorses.

He had not seen them the day before, perhaps because they'd been back in the trees in the pasture. He stood transfixed, in awe of their size. He had seen the other teams bringing the women, but he'd been well off to the side of the yard. Now he was almost directly beneath them and it was like looking up at giants.

He did not feel afraid. Something about them seemed gentle, peaceful, and he stood studying them, looking at their feet, which were a foot across, and their shoulders and the muscles in their sides . . .

"She has good horses, Kristina," one of the women said, standing next to him with a bucket of milk she had just filled. She was thin and had a little gray in her hair and small lines at the sides of her eyes from smiling. All the women seemed to have the lines from smiling. "Always the Jorgensons have had good horses. Good men and good horses." She turned and said, "Come, the milking is done and we have to turn the cows out and get back to the house," and walked to the other end of the barn while the other woman released the cows. The cows backed out of their stanchions and made their way carefully back to the pasture.

It was evening and the boy was very tired—not so long ago he had been young enough to take afternoon naps. But it was still light, the sun well up.

Maybe, he thought, he could stay out all night. Maybe he could sleep in the barn. Cowboys did it—in one of the Roy Rogers movies, he'd seen that cowboys slept in the barn. They ate from metal plates filled with brown beans and slept in the barn with their horses, and their hats over their faces, and their saddle for a pillow. He could try that—if he had a saddle and a hat to put over his face.

The house didn't seem to be a place for him, but only meant for women. He'd never thought of it that way, about there being places for men or boys and women or girls. There had always been just his mother and some-times his aunt Evelyn and of course his grandmother and him. Just all one thing.

But if those women could sit and make jokes about the sound that came from the upstairs bedroom he wasn't sure he was supposed to be there. He walked with the dog toward the house, but slowly.

The gray-haired woman turned and saw him stop-ping and seemed to know what he was thinking. "Come along. We have to eat supper and get some sleep to do chores tomorrow. Don't worry, Kristina is resting. She needs all the rest she can get because she has many hours of work to do."

He followed her then and decided he would just stay inside to eat, and if they started joking about the sound again, he would look for a hat and go back to the barn to sleep.

But the women were not joking now. He sat on a chair in the corner of the kitchen and they worked, cooking and filling pans with hot water and making bread, and he thought he had never seen so much food. Meat and potatoes and loaf upon loaf of bread, each wrapped in waxed paper and put in a metal bread box, and even after they ate and he was so full he could hardly walk, there was still more food left.

After the meal they made coffee in a big pot on the hottest center part of the woodstove by just dumping a handful of coffee grounds into boiling water and then adding some broken eggshells.

He did not understand the eggshells and thought it might have something to do with the baby, and because his grandmother was still gone with Martha and Kristina and because the woman in the barn had talked to him he asked her, "Are the eggshells to help the baby?"

She laughed, but not in a bad way, and ruffled his hair. "The eggshells take the bitterness out of the coffee. Here, try a sip."

He took a mouthful from her cup, which seemed so hot it must be on fire and so bitter he almost threw up. "How can you drink that?"

She laughed again. "After a while you can't live without it, eh, girls?" And she turned to the other women, holding her cup up to nods and smiles, then back to the boy. "You'll come to like it when you grow to like grown-up things."

Then there was a quiet time. The dishes were done and he had helped to wipe them. He felt that he should do something more but there wasn't anything he really knew how to do. They set him to filling the wood box next to the stove and he brought the wood in four pieces at a time until it was heaping and then went back to his chair in the corner to be out of the way.

His grandmother came down then and said something in Norwegian to the group, and one of the women said in English:

"So how long since the last pain?"

His grandmother came over to him and kissed him on top of the head and held him, which felt very right. She said, "Over an hour. Perhaps it was just false labor."

"What's labor?" he asked, and they went back to speaking in Norwegian and he realized they did that when they were talking about things they didn't think he should hear.

But the one from the barn said, "It's not so good when they've had hard labor and then stop this way, is it?"

And his grandmother shook her head and looked down at the boy and answered in Norwegian again, with a little snap in the words so the woman from the barn said:

"I'm sorry but my Norski isn't so good. It gets rusty."

His grandmother sat at the table then and ate a plateful of food and drank hot coffee steaming from the cup. She smiled at the boy and said, "Little pitchers have big ears."

"So it will be a long night, do you think?" one of the other women asked.

"That's what Martha said."

"So if the night is long maybe it is we should do quilt stories?"

Which was the way the boy started to learn about the quilt.

Chapter Seven

There was a new, strange energy in the house that he had not felt or seen before. They ate again; he had never seen so much food so often. They ate all the time they weren't working. And they drank hot, scalding hot, coffee with eggshells in it and ate rolls and jelly and bread with honey and pie and cake and meat and potatoes. Breakfast lasted to what they called forenoon lunch and then to the middle meal of the day, called dinner, and then afternoon lunch and then the evening meal called supper and then what they called a snack before going to bed.

He had not seen the dark yet in this summer because

his grandmother put him to bed when it was still light—nine or ten o'clock and still light—and the sun came up before he awakened.

But this time it was different. After the evening snack the gray-haired woman put on yet another pot of coffee to boil, and when it was finished his grandmother gave him a cup of coffee with milk and sugar in it and set him in a corner on the wood box and even as late as it was he did not feel sleepy because of the excitement in the air.

The women cleared off the kitchen table and spread the four chairs out and in a circle around it, well away from the table, and brought in two more wooden boxes from the porch to sit on. Another woman got the sheet bag with the colored cloth in it and put it on the table, and for a moment they all sat in chairs or on boxes sipping coffee.

They seemed to be waiting for something, and at first the boy could not tell why they were waiting and then Martha came down the stairs and into the kitchen. She was wearing a man's work shirt over her dress and had the sleeves rolled up past her elbows and held a washbasin with cool water and a small cloth hanging on the side, and she looked very, very tired.

"How is our girl doing?" one of the women asked.

"Resting now. Sleeping. She's pretty tired but I think all right. Sometimes early labor like that is false. There are no new pains and everything feels positioned right. I don't know what to do but wait. I will have coffee now . . . oh, are we going to look at the quilt?" She had seen the bundle on the table. "Were you waiting for me?"

His grandmother stood and nodded and said, "Sometimes it is good to think of old things, old ways, and do the old stories when there is nothing to do but wait."

And now the gray-haired woman took a folded quilt from the bag and the women stood and put their cups down on the counter, well away from the table, and each took a portion of the quilt and spread it out so the table was under the center, and the boy stood up on the wood box so that he was higher than the quilt and could see that it was very large, almost as large as the center of the kitchen, and made of dozens of patches

of cloth, all cut square and all sewn in a plain, rectan-
gular pattern.

There was no real design to it, other than a simple
checkerboard pattern, each piece about six inches
square, and of all different colors.

Almost all the squares had words embroidered in the
middle and the boy wished he could read. He knew
the letters and could sound them out, and sometimes
if two or three of them ran together he could make
the sound of them, like *k-aaaaa-t* when he saw the
word *cat* spelled on a piece of paper, but long words
were hard for him and many of the words on the quilt
were long.

The quilt was spread out, held by the women. They
looked down at the cloth and then up at each other.
The room grew quiet, breathlessly silent, so the boy
could hear Kristina breathing as she slept upstairs, and
he looked at the women's hands holding the edges of
the quilt and none of them gripped hard but seemed
instead to almost caress the cloth and he knew that he
was seeing a sweet thing, a dear thing, like when his
mother's face was there looking down on him as he

awakened from a nap, or when his grandmother looked at him when she held him.

Love. He did not know for sure exactly what love was but his mother had said she loved him, and loved his father. And his grandmother had said she loved him when she had that soft look, and he thought of it now. Love, they loved the cloth, no, loved the quilt, no, loved each other. They loved each other and the quilt and the cloth and it meant something he didn't understand.

His grandmother said, "We haven't gotten together to look at the quilt for a long time. Was it four, no, five months ago when . . . when Pearl passed?"

One of the women started to say something in Norwegian and his grandmother held up her hand.

"In American, please. English. The boy does not speak Norski and I want him to hear about the quilt. It is his life too, the quilt, as it is all our lives. . . ."

"I said you were right. It was just after Pearl passed that we got together over to Martha's to look at the quilt. See, there's Pearl's patch right there, at the bottom."

His grandmother put her hand on a square of white

cloth and turned to the boy. "See here? This was a piece of Pearl's wedding dress she saved for the quilt."

"Where is Pearl?" the boy asked.

There was a moment of silence and then his grandmother said, "Why, she passed. She was old and she passed away last year, so we sewed the part of her wedding dress into the quilt."

He still did not quite understand what passing or passing away meant. "Why do people pass things just because they're old?"

Another moment of silence and then his grandmother smiled and touched his cheek. "Not passing things. She died, that's what passing away means. Pearl was in her eighty-second year when she died and we sewed this piece of her wedding dress that she saved into the quilt so we would never forget her."

He looked at the white piece of silken cloth sewn into the quilt with the name PEARL embroidered in the middle, and even without being able to read he began to understand.

"Pearl came from the old country and was so beautiful people named their children after her, hoping for her beauty, and she married Sigurd," the gray-haired woman said, "but either she couldn't have children or Sigurd was not able to father children. They made a good farm with a hundred and sixty acres of homestead land six miles south of here and had cattle and hogs and very good corn, but without young what is the use of it?"

And the women sat and held the quilt in their laps and nodded and listened. "Nothing is good without young . . . ," one of them said.

"But she was wise and knew that if she couldn't have one child, her own child, she could have all children and so she became mother to us all and in that time when things happened to us that we could not tell our own mothers we would talk to Pearl." And here her voice softened. "And when we had questions about courting or dressing or marriage, we could talk to Pearl."

There were more nods now, and sounds of assent.

"And when at last we were all grown and Pearl was old there wasn't a young girl or woman here or any-where else in this township who had not talked to Pearl and been told of helpful things by Pearl and so when she passed she did not have one child, she had many children. All of us here and all of our children and all of our men were her children, and that is the story of Pearl."

And the boy realized that they all knew the story already and remembered it from the little square of white cloth and that the gray-haired woman had been telling the story for him, just for him. When she finished there was a moment of silence while Martha went upstairs to check on Kristina and just as the boy was going to thank the woman for telling him the story Martha came back. A woman to his right cleared her throat. She was named Louisa and wore her gray hair in a bun the way his grandmother did.

"Here is the cloth from Sigurd's wedding suit," she said. "And Pearl sewed it in with her own hands when Sigurd passed. His heart stopped while he was cleaning the barn in his fifty-second year and Pearl lived thirty more years after him, and she told me there was not a day that she didn't miss him, so much was their love." She took a breath and whispered, "And that is the story of Sigurd, husband to Pearl, father to us all."

And there was quiet again while they all thought of Sigurd.

The boy looked at the patches of cloth differently now, all of them with names, and did not like himself, because he couldn't read and understand the names, and swore he would learn to read the best he could and know all the names and what they meant.

"Are they all gone?" he asked. "Are they all passed?"

And his grandmother nodded and he felt a great loss because he had not known them. He got off the wood box and went to the edge of the quilt and touched a piece of coarse wool sweater. In the middle it said KARL MATHISON and the boy whispered, "Who is this one?"

And his grandmother drew a breath, a quick intake of air, and said in a whisper, "That was my father, your great-grandfather, who passed long before you were born."

And he said, "Can I know about him?"

And she smiled and he saw a small tear in the corner of her eye and she said, "Come and sit on my lap and we will listen to Louisa tell the story of Karl, because Louisa is the best teller of all and my papa was the best man of all."

Chapter Eight

The boy would never know that magic again in the way it came that evening and night, while they waited for Kristina to make the sounds and he learned the stories of the quilt. He listened hard, though he was exhausted, and drank the coffee with milk and sugar and looked first at the quilt while Louisa talked, but then watched the faces and hands of the women holding the cloth and saw all of it there as well.

"Karl was from the north part of the old country, where the winters were harder than even here, and he had learned the ax and two-man bucksaw and was so big his hands would cover stove lids. But the woods were not for him because before he was fully grown the sea called him and he went for to fish in the banks, the Grand Banks between the old country and the new where the great cod were, to catch and salt and dry and make *lutefisk*. He fished from a great sailing schooner in the small dories and they talked of his catches, so huge they nearly sank his boat.

"Then he met Trina. She had many other suitors because she had dark hair and dark eyes, which were much prized, with everybody blond and light, and her beauty was such that he wanted to give up the sea, but he could not because the call was so strong. It was in his blood, you see, as it is in all the Mathison blood. They cannot leave the sea.

"But Trina married him anyway. Their love overcame the sea, and there were three children that lived. One was Gretchen, a girl of great beauty like her mother, and another, Alida"—here she paused and nodded to the boy's grandmother—"small and also of great beauty, and a boy named Gunnar, who went with his father and followed the sea. And it came that every summer when the light was long Karl and Gunnar would go for the banks on the schooner and every winter they would come back and sit by the fire with Trina, repairing nets.

"But early one summer there was a late spring Norther and the seas grew huge in the Banks. Karl and Gunnar both were lost and that is the story of Karl."

Here the boy saw his grandmother, who was crying softly, run her hand from the square with Karl's name on it to one next to it on which was embroidered the word GUNNAR and the boy looked at the faces of the other women.

Karl was there in their eyes while Louisa talked in the music of the old stories—and Pearl and all the ones who had passed and all the ones who would pass—and though he would never see the quilt again it would live with him forever.

He fell asleep in his grandmother's lap while Louisa was still telling stories and he vaguely felt her carry him to the soft bed and slept hard until just before dawn, when he heard the sound again from upstairs, only more piercing, and nothing could make him stay in the house.

He walked through the kitchen in his pajamas but all the women were up and dressed as though they had been up all night. They had a fire in the stove and were heating coffee and water and rinsing out rags in a large pan of hot water.

And the sound came again, louder, and he was frightened, but Louisa who had told the stories gave him a piece of bread with honey and smiled. She said: "Maybe the men should wait outside."

"Is Kristina going to be all right?" he asked, dreading the answer, and her smile widened.

"This is the way it works, having babies. We heat water and drink coffee and there is noise and then it is over. You mustn't worry. She'll be fine. She is a great, strapping girl. . . ."

Just then the sound came again, louder still, and he nearly took the screen door off getting outside, where he sat on the ground by the front gate with the dog leaning against him, feeding the dog bits of bread with honey on them while he waited for . . . he did not know exactly what.

He could still hear the sound, only greatly muffled

and ending in short gasps and grunts. He waited for it to stop—he didn't think men were supposed to hear such things. He was sure Roy Rogers and the Sons of the Pioneers would not have to hear them, and neither would any other men. And he realized, with something of a shock, that there were no men in these women's lives.

It was not like his mother's life. His father was in a place called Europe fighting in tanks against the enemy but his mother had other men in her life.

There were no men here. They had passed on or were gone like Kristina's husband, Olaf, who was fighting in the war. They were not here and the women were doing everything alone, even the man things—running the farms, driving the teams, all the hard work. Only the women and children. And while they seemed to like men and sometimes love them, which he could hear in their voices when they talked of Karl and Sigurd, they seemed to get along fine without them, and he petted the dog and wondered if Roy Rogers and the Sons of the Pioneers knew that they really weren't needed once they caught the rustlers.

He wasn't sure how long he sat petting the dog and not listening to the sounds as they grew closer and closer together, but he had just decided to take the dog and see if there was a small stream down in back of the barn where he could make stick and leaf boats to bomb with rocks when he realized the sounds had stopped altogether.

He stood, holding his breath, listening. He heard nothing for a full minute and then, in the quiet, the new cry of a baby, and moments later the screen door opened and his grandmother was there, smiling.

"Come inside," she called. "Come inside and see."

Chapter Nine

There came a time then of such gentle happiness, week folding on week until a month had passed, that he nearly forgot all the bad things in his life, like missing his mother, and his father having to fight, and just lived each day looking for what new thing would come.

He had never paid much attention to babies except to hear them cry on the elevated train in Chicago when he was going to the Cozy Corner bar with his mother. They always seemed loud and messy. But he liked this baby.

It was a boy, named Olaf after his father and his

grandfather—Olaf the grandfather who was gone now and whose name was on the quilt. When the boy had first gone into the house, into the kitchen, he had almost turned and ran out. There were rags everywhere, all messy and bloody, and women washing them out in the sink and singing and laughing and not seeming to care at all how it looked, and he thought at first that Kristina must be dead because how could she live after such a mess and then he wondered how hard it must be to have a baby. They must have done some terrible thing to her to get the baby out of her. He almost didn't dare to go up the stairs. "Ten pounds," Martha said, washing her hands at the sink. "As sure as I'm standing here, ten pounds; what a little lunker for a first baby." And that scared him more because he did not know what a lunker was, or how big babies should be if ten pounds was something called a lunker.

But when his grandmother led him up and into the bedroom it was all clean and the light was coming brightly through the windows and curtains, and Kristina lay back on her pillow looking very tired but very, very happy, smiling gently at the bundle that lay next to her on the bed.

He stopped by the door but she said, "Come, look at what caused all the noise," and he came over and she opened the blanket and his grandmother said, "He looks just like his father."

"Is his father all wrinkled like that?" he asked, and they both laughed, although he meant it. The baby was all red and wrinkled and so tiny it didn't seem possible it had been the only thing inside Kristina, and he had a dozen questions, but she was so tired and he was so amazed that here was a baby, a little boy named Olaf, that he simply stood, staring, until his grandmother took him by the hand.

"Come now, let Kristina and Olaf rest. They've had a big day."

And she led him away, back down into the kitchen where the women were still cleaning and there was still that mess that almost made him sick, so he went back outside with the dog and walked down in back of the barn and thought of how he was Roy Rogers and Jake was Roy's dog, Bullet, and they started looking for rustlers on the edge of the pasture where rustlers might be trying to hide.

And that led to searching for robber gangs who were raiding the settlement in one of the movies he saw, and that led to thinking that he and Jake were fighting the war in Europe, and soon the day went to chores time and he helped the women and the next day was the same, playing with Jake.

In four days Elmer came and took two of the women home and two days later a wagon came and took three more and only Louisa was left to help his grandmother with the chores and not long after that a day came when Kristina left the baby in a cradle and slowly came to the barn for chores.

By the end of two weeks it was like there had always been a baby and the boy had become stronger, so he not only kept the cats off the cows and carried the stools but carried the milk buckets to the end of the barn as well, only spilling a little when he emptied them into the milk can.

Then Louisa left and it was just the four of them. Each morning the boy would look into the cradle with his face close to the baby and one morning Olaf smiled at him and he knew it was a smile even though his grandmother said it was a burp grin.

Endless days of chores in the morning and helping his grandmother gather eggs and playing with Jake and the cats, who became enemies in Europe or rustlers that needed to be chased and cornered before they could run off with the ranch's cattle.

Once he asked his grandmother if he could have a metal plate and some beans to eat, and sleep in the barn with a hat over his face. And she found a can of pork and beans and an old felt hat and even though they had to use a horse collar for a pillow because they had no saddle the boy slept in the barn, or started to until there were some noises after dark, when he had the hat over his face, that he wasn't sure about and he and Jake came back to the house just in case it was something they couldn't handle. That was how he told it to his grandmother when he came back in after almost an hour in the dark barn wearing the too-large old felt hat and dragging the blanket.

"I wasn't sure I could handle whatever it was making the noise. You know, without a six-shooter."

And she smiled at Kristina, but they nodded at his explanation as he went in to his feather bed in the small room off the kitchen.

In the evenings they would sit at the table and Kristina would nurse the baby and he would not look, because he felt—for some reason that he did not understand—that he wasn't supposed to watch, and his grandmother would try to teach him a card game called whist, which she was supposed to be very good at but which he never quite understood. He got the suits and sort of understood the numbering but the face cards and rules were impossible for him, and in the end they wound up playing a game called war, where his grandmother would lay a card down without looking at it and he would do the same and whoever had the bigger card took what was called the trick.

And so because he questioned everything he asked why it was called the trick when it didn't seem very tricky, but she didn't quite know and just told him it was that way because it was that way.

Sometimes in the evenings Kristina would read the letters she got from Olaf, the father who was not fighting the war in Europe but was fighting in something called the Pacific.

The mail appeared in the mailbox at the end of the driveway once every three days because the only car available to deliver mail came from a town forty miles away and with gas rationing there couldn't be daily mail. So once every three days the boy would take Jake, whom he was starting to call Bullet, and he would mount his horse—a stick with a slightly curved "head"—and ride to the end of the driveway and bring back the mail, and almost every time there was a letter from Olaf.

The letters were all full of news about how hot it was and how bad the food was and how all they had to eat was rice and something called dunderfunk but never about the fighting or anything really bad, although there must have been more because sometimes Kristina would seem to skip whole sections and read to herself and blush so hard that even the top of her breast—where he didn't feel comfortable looking— would turn red.

Everything was just exactly as he thought things should be except he missed his mother and wanted to meet his father and then came a day he did not like to remember at all, or think about even when he was an old man looking back on the times when everything was perfect.

He was kneeling in the dirt making roads and fields with his wooden grader blade and Jake was watching him carefully, as though needing to correct him, when he heard the sound of a car.

At first he thought it was the mailman but it was not a mail day, and then he wondered if they had found some gasoline from the ration place but it was not that, either, because the car turned into the driveway and when it got close he could see that it was a newer car, shiny black.

It stopped in front of him and two men got out and one was a minister, which the boy knew because he had a white collar, and the other man was a soldier in a full-dress brown uniform with a brown leather belt, and they smiled at the boy and opened the gate and knocked on the door and his grandmother let them in and for a few seconds there was no sound at all.

Not a bird, not a breath, not a whisper and then the boy heard a scream worse than anything he'd heard when the baby came, and he ran to the house and burst into the kitchen, where the baby was in the cradle and his grandmother was holding Kristina, who was sobbing, choking, fighting for air, panting and screaming all at once.

"We are very sorry for your loss," the soldier was saying—and his voice was even and his eyes tired, as if he had said this same thing many times and did not like having to say it—"and it is important for you to know that your husband gave his all for his country. . . ."

"My husband"—Kristina took a breath and raised her head, and the boy had never seen eyes like hers, hard and cold and full of tears and cornered and vicious—"is *dead*, you son of bitch! He has never seen his son and he is *dead!*"

"You must go now," his grandmother said to the men, taking Kristina back in her arms. "You have done your job and we must do ours now. Go."

The minister held out his hand but the boy's grandmother shook her head. "Thank you for doing your job but you must go now."

And they left and the boy stood, feeling a great loss he did not understand because he had not known Olaf the father. Yet something had been taken from his life.

And Kristina kept saying over and over, "What will I do, what will I dowhatwillIdowhatwillIdo," in a kind of sobbing song, and finally his grandmother held her at arms' length and shook her.

"You will do what we always do because we are women. You will raise your son because that is what we do. We are the strong ones, we have always been the strong ones. Men are weak and go off and fight or fish or work and do not come back, but we are women and we are strong because we go on. We always go on." And his grandmother was crying now as well, but her voice was hard and she shook Kristina again. "We go on and on when the men are gone. We keep them in the quilt and go on and on because in the end, when it is done, we are the only ones. We are the strong ones. Now pick up your baby and feed him and then clean the buckets because it is nearly chores time and we must work."

And she turned and threw the buckets in the sink and then faced the boy, who was standing by the door crying, and she said, her voice still hard, "Go and open the barn and let the cows in and get the stools down and we will come and milk. We must work. We must go on and we must work. Go now!"

After

Sitting in the little house in town coming into evening after apple pie and a glass of whole milk while his grandmother sips Norwegian coffee through a sugar lump, a time of questions:

"Will Olaf the father be in the quilt?"

"Of course. As was *his* father. In a few weeks when Kristina is a little stronger we will all get together and take the quilt out there and put Olaf into it."

"What will the quilt story say about him?"

"It will say the truth. The quilt always says the truth. That he was a good man who loved his family and wanted to be with them but the war took him. The quilt will tell the truth."

"Will my father pass over fighting in Europe?" He could not bring himself to use the word *killed*. It had been much on his mind since the two men had come to tell Kristina about Olaf, and he had even had a dream where his mother was in the apartment by the elevated railway in Chicago and the same two men came to her and he was not there to help her. "Will he pass over?"

"You mustn't think such things because there is no way to know."

"If he passes over will he be in the quilt?"

"Of course."

"If I pass over will I be in the quilt?"

"Of course."

"And Mother?"

"Of course."

"And you?"

She smiled. "I already have the piece of cloth from my wedding dress with my name on it."

"But not for a long time. You won't go on the quilt for a long time. And neither will Mother or Father or me."

"No. Not for a very long time. Now, you wash for bed and get your pajamas on and I'll tell you a story about a cow that glowed in the dark."

"Not really."

"Yes, really. Now go wash."

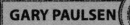
HOW TO SUCCEED
AND *SURVIVE* IN BUSINESS!

All I wanted was a way to make a little extra summer cash and mowing lawns seemed like a pretty easy way to do it. Who knew that climbing on my grandpa's old mower would change my life forever?

www.randomhouse.com/kids   WENDY LAMB BOOKS   RHCB

WELCOME TO THE WONDERFUL WORLD OF PUBERTY!

In this hilarious, honest, and ultimately optimistic book, Newbery Award–winning author Gary Paulsen puts his survival expertise to use against the most frightening wilderness of all—puberty!

Dare to explore: log on to
www.randomhouse.com/teens
for a complete list of books
by Gary Paulsen!

GARY PAULSEN IS ADVENTURE

AVAILABLE WHEREVER BOOKS ARE SOLD.

161

Illustrations © Souther Salazar.

RANDOM HOUSE CHILDREN'S BOOKS

WENDY LAMB BOOKS